JAN - - 2018

SL:4.4
AR:2

THE *VANISHING* TREASURE

STONE ARCH BOOKS
a capstone imprint

SNOOPS, INC. IS PUBLISHED BY
STONE ARCH BOOKS, A CAPSTONE IMPRINT
1710 ROE CREST DRIVE
NORTH MANKATO, MINNESOTA 56003
WWW.MYCAPSTONE.COM

Printed and bound in Canada 10041S17

Library of Congress Cataloging-in-Publication Data
Names: Terrell, Brandon, 1978– author. | Epelbaum, Mariano, 1975– illustrator.
Title: The Vanishing Treasure / by Brandon Terrell ; illustrated by Mariano Epelbaum.
Description: North Mankato, Minnesota : Stone Arch Books, a Capstone imprint,
[2017] | Series: Snoops, Inc.
Identifiers: LCCN 2016033022 (print) | LCCN 2016035071 (ebook) |
ISBN 9781496543455 (library binding) | ISBN 9781496543493 (paperback) |
ISBN 9781496543615 (eBook PDF)
Subjects: LCSH: Theft—Juvenile fiction. | Contests—Juvenile fiction. |
Twins—Juvenile fiction. | Brothers and sisters—Juvenile fiction. |
African American girls—Juvenile fiction. | Hispanic American boys—Juvenile fiction. |
Friendship—Juvenile fiction. | Detective and mystery stories. |
CYAC: Mystery and detective stories. | Stealing—Fiction. | Contests—Fiction. |
Twins—Fiction. | Brothers and sisters—Fiction. | African Americans—Fiction. |
Hispanic Americans—Fiction. | Friendship—Fiction. | GSAFD: Mystery fiction. |
LCGFT: Detective and mystery fiction.
Classification: LCC PZ7.T273 Van 2017 (print) | LCC PZ7.T273 (ebook) |
DDC 813.6 [Fic]—dc23
LC record available at https://lccn.loc.gov/2016033022

BY BRANDON TERRELL

**ILLUSTRATED BY
MARIANO EPELBAUM**

EDITED BY: AARON SAUTTER
BOOK DESIGN BY: TED WILLIAMS
PRODUCTION BY: STEVE WALKER

FREE *WRITING WORKSHOP!*

SNOOPS INC.

"NO CASE TOO SMALL... WE SOLVE THEM ALL!"

IF YOU'VE GOT A MYSTERY TO SOLVE

WE'LL FIND THE CLUES

TO CRACK THE CASE FOR YOU!

THEN GIVE US A CALL

688-CLUB | 688-CLUB | -CLUB | 688-CLUB | 688-CLUB | 688-CLUB

CALLING ALL MAGICIANS!

JOIN THE MAGIC CLUB!

IT'S MATH-TASTIC!

Cheer on the Fleischman Math team as they go for their 5th straight championship!

SATURDAY, MARCH 12
10 AM – 3 PM

LOCATED AT HAYNES COMMUNITY COLLEGE

SNOOPS INC.

ZIPPY 'ZA

PETS GALORE

HENSON PARK

DIAZ GROCERIES

CHAPTER 1

TO CATCH A THIEF

From their perch on the apartment building's old metal fire escape, the two boys had a perfect bird's-eye view of Henson Park near their home. It was growing dark, and the city began to glow with street lamps and brightly-lit windows. Curfew time crept up on them as they patiently sat on one of the fire escape's platforms, their legs dangling out into thin air.

Twelve-year-old Jaden Williams scoped
out the scene as a few people walked or jogged
through the tree-filled park. For the most
part, though, it was empty. The only bike at
the rack was Jaden's pride and joy, a shiny red
speedster. The bike had no lock on it, but not
because Jaden had forgotten it.

He'd left it unlocked on purpose.

Beside Jaden, fourteen-year-old Carlos Diaz
stared through a pair of old binoculars he had
borrowed from his dad. Carlos spoke into the
earpiece attached to his phone by a thin cord.
"Eyes in the Sky here, nothing yet."

Hayden Williams looked up from the book she
was reading by a nearby streetlight. Hayden,
Jaden's twin sister and older by twelve minutes,
sat on a park bench. An earpiece was stuck in one
of the sixth-grader's ears, the cord snaking down
to her own phone.

Hayden quietly said, "Same here. All quiet on
the park bench front."

On the other side of the park, near a bubbling stone fountain, thirteen-year-old Keisha Turner stopped jogging. She'd been casually running circles around the park and stopped now to pull back her thick curls in a ponytail and re-tie her left sneaker.

The seventh-grade girl spoke into her own hidden earpiece. "Copy that," Keisha said. "Maybe we should call it. Pack up and go home. This stakeout is a bust."

As if on cue, Carlos saw something in his binoculars. A figure, cloaked in shadow, was skulking behind a nearby tree. "Hold up," the eighth-grader said. "I think we've got something."

"Roger that, Eyes in the Sky," Hayden said. She pretended to read again, but kept an eye on Jaden's bike.

Keisha straightened up and began to jog again.

Jaden leaned forward, worried about his bike. "It's gonna be okay, right?" he asked Carlos. "I mean, I saved up to buy that bad boy for over a year. I lost count of all the dogs I walked and other odd jobs I did. I didn't do all that work just to use my bike as a piece of bait."

"It'll be fine, Jaden," Carlos assured him.

The figure behind the tree carefully looked both ways, saw the coast was clear, and slipped out from the shadows.

It was a girl, maybe a couple of years older than the junior detectives staking out the park. The girl hurried forward, moving right for the bike.

"Looks like the reports of a bicycle thief were right," Hayden whispered under her breath. She watched as the girl quickly backed Jaden's bike out of the rack and leapt aboard.

"My baby!" Jaden squealed.

Carlos clapped a hand over Jaden's mouth. "Be cool," he hissed.

The girl, not hearing Jaden's cry, began to furiously pedal off down one of the park's empty paths. She whizzed past Keisha without a second glance at the jogger.

"Hayden, you ready?" Keisha asked.

"Yup." Hayden closed her book and calmly set it on the bench beside her. The girl on the stolen bike was coming up fast. Hayden popped a grape sucker into her mouth and pulled a small device from her pocket.

The girl on the bike raced down the sidewalk. She was thirty yards from Hayden. Twenty . . . ten . . . five.

Hayden pressed a button on her device. *Screeeeech!*

The bike came to a sudden, stuttering stop right in front of Hayden. The thief flew forward and struck the handlebars of the bike. "Oof!" she cried as the wind was dashed from her lungs.

Hayden watched as the thief lifted her leg over the bike and dismounted. Dazed, the thief staggered away. The bike dropped to its side on the sidewalk.

Hayden slid over. "Ouch! I bet that hurt. Here," she said, patting the wooden bench beside her. "Need a seat?"

The thief plopped down on the bench.

Jaden and Carlos clambered down the fire escape and dashed to the scene. While Carlos headed directly to Hayden and the thief, Jaden slid to his knees beside his fallen bike.

"My precious," he said, lifting the bike and holding it gently. "It's gonna be okay, I promise. You're not hurt, are you?"

"Your bike is fine, ya goofball," Hayden said. She pointed at the bike's rear wheel. A small, U-shaped device was secured to it. "And my ghost brakes clamped down just like I planned."

"Looks like you've snatched your last bike," Carlos said to the winded thief. Keisha strolled up behind Carlos, resting one arm on his shoulder and leaning against him. She had her phone in her other hand and was placing a call.

"Yeah, police?" she said. "You know that bike thief you're looking for? Well she's just been busted by Snoops, Incorporated."

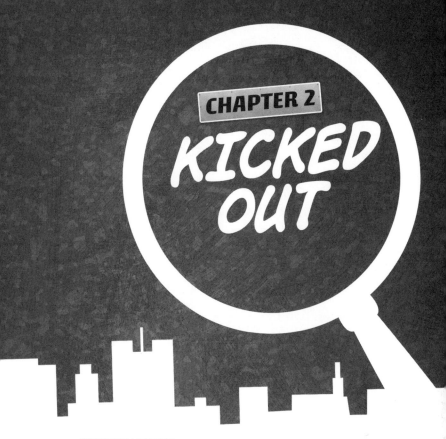

SUPERSNOOPER: *Are u as excited about the Math-Tastic meet this weekend as I am?*

MARPLE_FAN: *Oh yeah. More, probably. You're going down! ¡^)*

Hayden let out a short burst of laughter. Her fingers danced across her phone, furiously typing as she walked through Fleischman Middle School. Classes had ended for the day, but some students still roamed the old, brick hallways.

Hayden had never met Marple Fan, whose screen name came from the famous detective character Miss Marple. The two were both members of the Young Forensics Club, an online group devoted to discussing tips and tricks used to solve crimes and mysteries. YFC members lived all over the country (and one member, Slapshot_P.I., even lived in Canada).

Hayden had recently learned that not only was Marple Fan from the same city as her, they were both math leaguers! The two middle schoolers would be facing off at the regional Math-Tastic event at Haynes Community College.

SUPERSNOOPER: *LOL! Watch it Marple_Fan! It's gonna be insane. Can't wait to finally meet!*

MARPLE_FAN: *Right back at ya!*

Hayden hurried to the Fleischman media center. Math-Tastic practice started in ten minutes, and she didn't want to be late. The coach, Miss Kahin, was strict about being on time.

As she breezed into the media center, Hayden came to an abrupt stop. The Math-Tastic team was huddled just inside the door . . . so close that she almost ran into the back of the nearest student.

"Whoa!" Hayden yelled instinctively.

The boy she'd almost run into was an eighth-grader named Tuam Li. Tuam was tall and thickset. He wore a grey cardigan and an *Invasion From Planet X* T-shirt. "Oh, hey Hayden," he whispered when he turned and saw her.

Hayden looked past Tuam. "What's going on?" she asked.

"Miss Kahin told us to stay over here," Tuam explained. "We're waiting for the all-clear."

"What's she doing?"

"Pretty sure Warren Garvey's getting the boot," a voice said from the front of the crowd. Frankie Dixon, school snob extraordinaire and Keisha's ex-bestie, leaned against a bookshelf. The seventh-grade girl clutched a ridiculously bright and glittery notebook to her chest with both arms.

"The boot?" Hayden asked. "Like . . . he's getting kicked out? But Warren is the reigning Math-Tastic champ."

"Yeah," Frankie replied impatiently, rolling her eyes. "And it looks like a repeat victory isn't going to happen. Of course, we'd know for sure if you stopped yammering and let us listen."

Frankie was easily the most obnoxious girl Hayden knew. How Keisha had ever been best friends with her was a mystery even Snoops, Inc. couldn't solve. Of course, Hayden also couldn't figure out how Frankie had even made it onto the Math-Tastic team in the first place.

Hayden held her tongue. Arguing with Frankie never solved anything.

As the group quieted down, Miss Kahin's stern voice could be heard coming from the closed door of the media center's study room. "I'm sorry, Warren," she said. "But I spoke with both Principal Snider and your history teacher. We all came to the decision together."

"Y-y-you can't kick me out of math league," Warren stammered. "I didn't mean to cheat on that test. I just . . . I'm under a lot of stress. I-I-I'm sorry, Miss Kahin." Hayden could hear the panic and anger in Warren's voice and imagined the boy was near tears.

"I'm sorry, too," Miss Kahin said. "I wish your career as a Math-Tastic member didn't have to end like this. I'm also very disappointed. Now if you'll excuse me, the rest of the team is waiting to practice."

"Everyone be cool," Tuam said. "Here he comes." He snatched a book off the nearest shelf and pretended to read it. He apparently didn't notice it was upside-down. Others messed with their phones or tablets.

A moment later, Warren strode around the farthest bookshelf and into sight. The eighth-grade student stopped when he saw the team. The lanky boy had thick brown hair. His eyes were red and swollen.

Hayden felt a twinge of sadness for the disgraced math champ.

Warren dropped his head and continued toward the door. As he passed the team, he muttered angrily, "Good luck without me." Then he banged open the door and exited the media center.

"Well that was awkward," Frankie Dixon said, shaking her head.

The team moved as one into the media center. As they reached the study room with its glass walls, Hayden saw Miss Kahin standing at the long table with her head down. The colorful blue sash draped from her shoulder to her waist appeared to highlight her somber mood. The Somali teacher had both hands on the table in a pose that made her look devastated.

However, when the team entered the room, Miss Kahin's head lifted and a large, fake smile was plastered on it. "Greetings, everyone," she said. "Ready for this weekend's competition?"

A round of "Yeahs," and "You know its," filled the room as the Math-Tastic team sat at the table. Hayden slipped into a chair beside Tuam, removing her calculator and tablet from her backpack.

"Now," Miss Kahin continued. "Before we start, let's clear the air. I know you all just heard my conversation with Warren. It's unfortunate, but cheating is grounds for immediate removal from the team. If we're going to get our name etched onto the Math-Tastic trophies, we're going to do it with honest, hard work."

She snatched a stack of papers off the desk and cleared her throat. "Okay, now that we've got that ugly business out of the way, let's do some practice tests."

Miss Kahin began passing out the packets filled with word problems similar to those the team would see during the competition. Hayden glanced out the nearest window.

From it, she could see the sidewalk outside Fleischman, the busy street, and the row of brick buildings beyond.

Standing on the far sidewalk, staring back at the school angrily, was Warren Garvey.

Hayden quickly picked up her tablet, opened the link to her YFC account, and sent Marple Fan a note.

SUPERSNOOPER: *You're never gonna believe what just happened.*

CHAPTER 3
LET THE GAMES BEGIN!

"Come on, Jaden! I'm gonna be late!"

Hayden pounded on the closed bathroom door.
Saturday mornings were usually a quiet, peaceful
time for the family. Hayden and Jaden would
kick back and watch cartoons while their parents
enjoyed a pot of coffee and a crossword puzzle.

This particular Saturday morning was
different. Hayden had to be at Haynes

Community College in less than an hour for the Math-Tastic competition.

"Jaden!" Hayden knocked louder.

"All right, all right." Jaden swung open the bathroom door. He wore a bulky blue robe. A baseball cap was perched atop his mess of wet hair, and he had a deck of playing cards in his hand.

Hayden scrunched up her face at the sight of the cards. "What are you doing in there?"

"Oh, you know," Jaden said smugly, shuffling the cards in his hands. "Just practicing my newest magic act."

"In the bathroom? Gross."

"Hey. A magician does what it takes to perfect his craft."

"Whatever." Hayden shoved past him and into the bathroom.

Twenty minutes later, she and her mom were walking briskly out of the apartment building. "Did you eat anything?" her mom asked, sipping from a giant travel mug of coffee as they crossed the intersection.

Hayden shook her head.

As they passed Diaz Groceries, the small store run by Carlos' family, her mom nodded at the baskets of fresh produce. "Maybe you should grab something," she said. Mr. Diaz stood nearby, stocking avocados and whistling.

Hayden chose a large apple from one of the displays. Mr. Diaz saw them and waved. "Morning!" he said. "Big day today, huh? Carlos told me about the competition."

"Yep," Hayden said. "Math-Tastic, here I come!"

Her mom dug in her pocket for some cash to pay for the apple. Mr. Diaz waved her off. "The brain fuel is on the house," he said.

Hayden thanked him, and they continued on their way.

Haynes Community College was a small campus set in the heart of the city. Hayden had been past it many times; the art museum her mom loved to visit was only a block away. Haynes was made up of four old, stone buildings connected by hallways, forming a giant U. In the middle was a small, grass-filled courtyard that held a tall bronze statue of a woman reaching for the sun.

"Good luck today, sweetie," Hayden's mom said as she stopped on the sidewalk in front of the college. She kissed Hayden on the forehead. "You'll do great. And remember, no matter what, you're a genius in my book."

"Thanks, Mom." Hayden gave her a quick hug, then hurried on alone.

Haynes' math and science building was easy to spot; it was swarming with people. Hayden saw Tuam standing outside, backpack slung over his shoulder, looking like he'd just arrived as well.

"Hey!" Hayden jogged over to catch him.

"Have you seen the rest of the team?" Tuam asked her.

Hayden shook her head. "They must already be inside."

The two filtered into the math building with a number of other kids. As they entered the lobby, they saw many kids already heading toward the building's large ballroom, where students were splitting into their separate teams. Hayden wondered if Marple Fan was here yet. Heck, she could have just passed her online pal and she wouldn't have known it.

On the far side of the lobby, away from the hubbub of activity, was a trophy case. Hayden began to walk toward the case instead of heading into the ballroom. Tuam followed her.

The case contained shelves of glittering gold and silver trophies locked behind a pane of glass. There were trophies and plaques in all shapes and sizes. The two Math-Tastic trophies sat on the top shelf. They were identical; each had a pillar of glittering blue and red topped with a golden calculator. The only difference between the trophies was the large plates on the base. One contained the etched names of previous winning teams. The other held the names of students who took top honors each year.

"Think we have a shot at bringing them back to Fleischman?" Tuam asked. Every year, the winning school took the trophies home. They

were then returned to the college's trophy case the week before the next competition.

Hayden looked closely at the plate on the team trophy. Fleischman Middle School had won the last several competitions. Their name appeared one year after the next.

"It's gonna be tough without Warren," Hayden replied as she spied her ex-teammate's name on the individual trophy.

"Psst!" Tuam elbowed her. "Check it. There's Newt Loggins."

Hayden turned. Nearby, she saw a boy in a plaid button-down shirt tucked into khaki pants, with a polka-dot bow tie and a pocket square. Newt was from a school named Eastern Prep. He had taken second place at the previous year's regional competition, losing out to Warren Garvey.

"Excuse me," a short, stocky boy said as he brushed past them. He wore a backpack and carried a battered paperback book in one hand.

"Hey, Martin," Tuam said to the boy.

Martin turned, gave a curt wave, and continued on his way.

"Martin Reynolds," Tuam explained. "He just transferred to Watson. Quiet dude."

Watson Middle School was Fleischman's biggest rival. They often competed against one another in sports and academics. Of course, Fleischman usually beat them, but the two schools had been battling for decades.

The crowd in the lobby was waning as most kids made their way into the packed ballroom. Hayden and Tuam joined them.

Tables had been set up around the walls of the ballroom for each team. A large stage with chairs and desks had been erected for students to sit at as they competed. Rows of folding chairs faced the stage.

Hayden and Tuam found Miss Kahin and the remainder of the Fleischman team in their designated section of the ballroom.

"What took you so long?" Frankie Dixon asked. She was seated in one of the red folding chairs, chomping gum loudly.

Hayden ignored the question, instead turning to Miss Kahin. "How long before the first match?" she asked.

Miss Kahin checked her watch. "Forty-five minutes," she said. "You're in the first group."

Students from each team took turns competing over several rounds. The final round, called the Countdown Competition, was completed by the top eight students. Individual scores were then tallied to determine the Math-Tastic champion.

Hayden found a seat against the wall. She stuck a grape sucker in her mouth and buried her nose in a practice test, blocking out the rest of the crowd while she prepared.

"Mind if I sit here?"

Hayden didn't know how long she'd been studying before the voice broke her from her math trance. She looked up and saw a girl with shoulder-length black hair standing in front of her.

"Um, yeah," Hayden said, dazed. "I mean, no . . . I don't mind."

The girl sat down, leaning back against the wall. "I'm Anya," she said, smiling. "Anya Stavos. I go to Watson."

"Oh. Hayden Williams. Fleischman."

"You mean you're the enemy?" Anya furrowed her brow, pretending to be angry.

Hayden laughed. "The one and only."

"Sorry if I broke your concentration," Anya said. "I'm super nervous. This is my first Math-Tastic competition."

"It's cool. I get nervous too." Hayden pointed at the sucker turning her mouth purple. "This helps."

"Totally."

"You want one?"

"Sure."

She didn't know why, but for some reason, Hayden felt comfortable around Anya. It was almost like they knew each other already. They were talking like old friends. It felt a lot like the way she spoke to —

Marple Fan?

She didn't say it out loud, but she suddenly had the urge to ask. It couldn't be that easy, though, could it?

Hayden passed a sucker to Anya. She wanted to say something, to ask if her new friend was actually her online friend. But before she could, a concerned woman came striding into the ballroom. She had a clipboard in one hand and a lanyard with a tag reading "Official" on it hanging from her neck. The woman's eyes flitted about until she saw Miss Kahin. She hurried over.

"Excuse me," the woman said, trying to be discreet and failing. "Where are the trophies?"

Miss Kahin looked puzzled. "What do you mean? I brought them back last week. They're in the trophy case."

The woman shook her head. "They most certainly are not," she said.

Hayden quickly stood. Something was wrong.

"I . . . I don't understand," Miss Kahin said.

"Follow me," the woman said.

She led Miss Kahin back toward the lobby area. As Hayden watched them go, Tuam stepped up beside her. "What's going on?" he asked.

"It's the trophies," Hayden said. "They're missing!"

CHAPTER 4

GATHERING CLUES

Hayden was sitting in the shade of the bronze statue in the college's courtyard when the rest of Snoops, Inc. arrived on the scene. She had called them shortly after hearing about the missing trophies. Carlos and Keisha breezed in on their bicycles, while Jaden carefully rode down the sidewalk on his brand-new red bike.

"Easy now," Jaden said as he applied the brakes and came to a delicate stop. He looked around at some of the other students who had made their way out onto the grassy courtyard. After the discovery of the missing trophies, the Math-Tastic competition had been delayed. "What's up, sis?"

"Yeah, what's going on, Hayden?" Carlos asked, getting right to business. As the leader of Snoops, Inc., he often took charge of the situation.

Hayden told them everything she knew, how she and Tuam had personally seen the trophies in the case, and how they were now missing.

"Can we see the scene of the crime?" Carlos asked.

"Sure," Hayden said. "Come on."

The junior detectives parked their bikes at a rack nearby. Jaden took extra care when locking his up. Hayden led the way to the lobby area of the math building. Several officials huddled near the entrance to the ballroom. No one guarded the trophy case, which was both good and bad. If there were any clues, they could be contaminated. Still, Snoops, Inc. needed to take a look.

Keisha took out her phone and fired up the camera app.

"Looks like the case has a lock on it," Carlos said, examining the glass door. "I don't see any signs of forced entry. Or any smudges or fingerprints on the glass."

"So either the thief had a key . . . " *Click*! Keisha snapped a photo. "Or the case wasn't locked."

"Did you check it when you looked at the trophies?" Jaden asked.

Hayden rolled her eyes. "Of course not."

Carlos continued to search around the trophy case. A tall, potted plant sat along the wall nearby. He dropped to one knee. "Guys! I've got something."

The others crowded around him. On the floor was a crumpled up packet of paper. It looked like a Math-Tastic practice test.

"Dude," Jaden said. "You found garbage. Way to go."

Carlos shook his head. "You never know," he said. "Every clue counts."

Jaden stepped forward and began to reach for the paper. "It's not a clue," he said.

"Wait!" Hayden stopped him. "Carlos is right. Treat it like a clue."

Keisha was already one step ahead of her. She unzipped the small pack she carried and removed a plastic bag.

"Don't get your prints all over it," Hayden said.

"Okay, okay," Jaden said. Then his eyes lit up. "If only I had a handkerchief!"

With his left hand, he dramatically reached into the right sleeve of his hoodie. From it, he withdrew a red hankie.

"What is that?" Hayden asked.

Jaden said nothing. As he continued to pull, the hankie turned blue. Then green. Yellow. Purple. Orange. Red again.

"*Voilá!*" he shouted, pulling the last of the hankie from his sleeve. It fluttered through the air and drifted to the floor.

The other three Snoops stared at him blankly.

"You guys are the worst," Jaden grumbled. He picked a corner of the handkerchief, used it to pinch the edge of the paper packet, and dropped it into the bag.

"Hayden!" Tuam was exiting the ballroom, waving in her direction. "Miss Kahin wants you. The officials decided to continue with the competition while security looks for the trophies. The first round is gonna start in ten minutes."

"Oh no! That's not much time." In all the excitement, Hayden had forgotten she was competing in the first round.

"Good luck," came a voice from behind her. Anya Stavos was walking through the lobby area, a smile on her face. Her Watson teammate, Martin Reynolds, walked alongside her.

"Thanks," Hayden said.

As the other competitors hurried back into the ballroom, Hayden stayed for a moment longer to speak with her friends.

"Okay, so while I'm completing the first round, you guys keep looking around for clues," she said.

"Sure thing," Carlos said.

"Clues like this?" Keisha was bending over, already snapping photos of something on her phone. They hadn't noticed it before, but part of the carpeting near where they were standing was smudged. Dark grime, almost like oil, and particles of sawdust were pressed into the carpet.

"Were those there a minute ago?" Carlos asked.

Jaden shrugged. "First time I'm seeing them."

"This is weird," Carlos said. "We've got a mystery, but we don't have a suspect."

"I've got a suspect for you." Frankie Dixon stood in the lobby area. Her sudden appearance made the Snoops jump back in surprise.

"Frankie! Hey . . ." Jaden quickly adjusted his ball cap, trying to play it cool. He had a serious crush on Frankie, one that kind of made Hayden want to throw up a little.

"You have a suspect?" Carlos asked.

"Well, you're trying to find who took the trophies, right?" Frankie asked.

Carlos nodded.

"Then I know who did it. It's easy. I saw him by the trophy case earlier this morning."

"Who'd you see?" Keisha asked directly.

A sly smile curled one corner of Frankie's mouth. "None other than Warren Garvey."

CHAPTER 5

A SKETCHY SITUATION

"Warren Garvey?" Hayden blurted out.

"Who's Warren Garvey?" Keisha asked.

"He's the reigning Math-Tastic champ —"
Hayden began.

"— who was just kicked off the team for
cheating," Frankie finished.

Carlos perked up at this news. "Interesting,"
he said. "How did he react?"

Hayden recalled Warren, tearful and angry, banging his way out of Fleischman's media center. "Not well," she said.

"Then that would totally give him a motive for wanting to steal the trophies." Carlos said.

"Really?" Jaden was back to shuffling his deck of cards, like a nervous tic.

"People have done worse for less," Carlos answered.

Tuam appeared in the ballroom doorway again, waving a meaty hand in the air frantically.

"I gotta jet," Hayden said. "For real, this time. You guys search for Warren, see if he's still around."

"He went that way," Frankie said. She pointed down a nearby hall. A sign above it showed that the hall led to the school's cafeteria and recreation center.

"We're on it," Carlos said. "Good luck."

Hayden sighed. "Thanks."

She was the last competitor to find a seat on the stage. Two students from each school were participating. Newt Loggins sat quietly lining up a handful of sharpened pencils. Anya Stavos gave Hayden a quick wave. Everyone was squirming and fidgeting in their chairs. They'd spent months getting ready for this important competition. The pressure they all felt was immense. Hayden could feel the anxiety begin to bubble up and tried hard to press it back down.

"Students will have fifteen minutes to complete as many questions as they can," a Math-Tastic official stated as he passed out closed test booklets.

A small buzzer sounded, and they were off!

Hayden tore open her booklet and readied her pencil. The first question read:

1. 288 minutes = ? % of a single day?

She began to scribble her work in one of the margins. As she did, though, she kept thinking about the missing trophies. *How could they have disappeared without anyone noticing? Where were they? And who took them?*

As her mind drifted, Hayden glanced up at the other students on the stage. They were all hunched over, all focused on their tests . . . except the guy Tuam had spoken about earlier, Martin Reynolds.

He was staring right at her. But when they locked eyes, Martin quickly looked away.

Hayden's pulse quickened. Something was strange, but she couldn't do anything about it now. She trained her attention back on the packet, and focused on answering the first question.

* * *

Twenty minutes later, Hayden was hurrying out of the ballroom when her phone chirped. She had an alert set on her YFC account for any time someone messaged her. It was no surprise that this particular message was from Marple Fan.

MARPLE_FAN: Heard about the missing trophies.
Snoops, Inc. on the case?

Hayden looked left and right, trying to see if any of the students milling about were also on their phone. Several were. Any of them could be Marple Fan, she supposed. But her gut was telling her it was Anya. Hayden needed to know.

The two had to meet. Hayden wrote back.

SUPERSNOOPER: You know it. I think we should meet.

MARPLE_FAN: Great idea! Cafeteria in 20 minutes?

Hayden replied yes, then headed off down the hall toward the cafeteria.

It wasn't until she smelled the delicious aromas coming from the cafeteria that she remembered how little she'd eaten that morning. The apple, or "brain fuel," as Mr. Diaz called it, had been tasty, but not fulfilling. She needed more.

Thankfully, her brother was one step ahead of her. As she walked into the cafeteria, she saw the other Snoops seated at a table near a wall of flashing arcade games. Jaden had a tray of food in front of him. How he was able to pack away so much food, Hayden would never know. Her brother's stomach was bottomless.

The cafeteria held several food stations, each serving a variety of lunch choices such as pizza, tacos, soups, and deli sandwiches. Attached to the cafeteria was the rec center, with its billiard and foosball tables. A number of students milled about. Hayden wove through the cafeteria tables until she reached her friends.

"How'd you do?" Carlos asked.

She shrugged, slipping into the booth beside Keisha. "Okay, I think. How'd *you* do? Any luck finding Warren?"

"Nope," Jaden said. He pushed his tray in her direction, offering her some food. She gladly took a slice of greasy pizza.

"So where do we go from here?" Keisha asked, also grabbing a slice.

As if in answer, Hayden felt a presence beside her. *Marple Fan*? she thought, looking up at the newcomer.

"Oh," she said, trying not to sound disappointed. "Um, hi."

Martin Reynolds stood beside the booth. He wrung his hands together nervously, looking down at Hayden the same way he'd peered at her during the competition.

"Hi," Martin said shyly. "Do you . . . have a minute?"

"Sure." Carlos stood and snatched a chair from a neighboring table. He pulled it over for Martin, and the two boys sat.

"What can we help you with?" Carlos asked.

"You guys are looking for the missing trophies, right?" Martin looked around, almost as if he expected someone to be listening in on their conversation.

"You know it," Jaden said.

"Okay, well, I saw something. Or someone, I guess."

"Hold up." Hayden unzipped her backpack and took out her tablet. The old device had seen better days, but it still purred like a kitten. She quickly unlocked the device with her password. "Could you describe this person?" she asked.

Martin shrugged. "I think so."

She opened an app on the tablet with one hand while grabbing another of her favorite grape suckers from her backpack with the other.

"What app is that?" Jaden asked, peering over her shoulder.

"It's called Sketch & Arrest," Hayden explained. "It creates composite sketches using a database of thousands of facial features."

"What's a composite sketch?" Jaden looked confused.

"It's like a police artist's drawing."

"Cool."

"Okay, Martin," Hayden said. "What can you tell me about the person you saw?"

As Martin Reynolds began to describe the mysterious stranger, Hayden tapped various options into the tablet. A blank face soon gained a pair of deep-set eyes. A long nose. Thin lips, a pointed chin, and a mop of brown hair.

"The exact details are a bit fuzzy," Martin said. "But yeah, that's close."

"This is a great start," Hayden said. "Thanks."

"Just trying to help," Martin said. He waved and slunk off back toward the math building.

Hayden showed the others the sketch on her tablet.

Jaden cocked his head to one side. "You know, Frankie might be right. It does kind of look like Warren Garvey."

"Maybe." Keisha didn't seem as convinced.

"How frequently do these sketches actually look like the culprit?" Jaden asked.

"You'd be surprised," Hayden answered.

"We should ask around about this sketch," Carlos suggested. "If that doesn't work, we should make copies and post them around the school. Like on that bulletin board." He gestured with his thumb toward the wall, where a large board with a number of colorful advertisements and posters hung. The ads covered everything from piano lessons to free tickets for open mic night at Chuckle Town Comedy Club.

The Snoops crew gathered their things. Then they went from table to table, showing the sketch to each person they saw. Most people shook their heads, politely saying they hadn't seen anyone with that description.

Hayden was about to give up when she reached a table where a pair of college guys with scraggly beards were seated. Both had trays heaped with food. "Excuse me," she said, showing them the tablet. "Have you seen anyone who looks like this?"

One of the guys glanced at the digital sketch. "Whoa," the guy said, his voice smooth and calm. "Totally. I saw that dude earlier. Had a bulky backpack and everything."

"Really?" Hayden asked, perking up. "Where did you see him?"

"Down by room 117," he said. Then, seeing the perplexed looks of the junior sleuths, he added, "The wood shop."

The other guy pointed down the hall farthest from them. "That way," he said.

"Thanks."

Heading in the direction of room 117, the young sleuths hurried off in search of their suspect.

CHAPTER 6

A MAGICAL LEAD

The sawdust, Hayden thought to herself as the Snoops made their way down the darkened hall. The smell of oil, grease, and wood filled the air, assaulting her nostrils.

"Look over here," she said, pointing to the carpeted floor. It was well-worn. Mixed into the faded gray carpet were bits of wood and sawdust, spots of grit and grime. "Remember the sawdust we found on the floor, near the trophy case?"

"It must have come from the wood shop," Keisha said.

"So do you think the trophies are here?" Carlos asked.

"One way to find out." Hayden shouldered open the heavy door to room 117.

The wood shop was dark and empty. A row of windows high on the wall cast beams of light down into the space. Sawdust swirled about, caught in the glow like fireflies. Cumbersome table saws, band saws, and drill presses filled the shop, along with a series of wooden tables and stools for students.

Hayden searched about, looking among the machinery for the trophies. Nothing. No glittering gold was to be found.

However, there was something else.

"Guys!" she shouted, waving them over. She stood in the back of the room, near a table saw. Perched atop it, gleaming brightly in a shaft of light, was a pile of items.

"A backpack," Carlos said.

"A wig," Keisha noted.

"And a . . . mask?" Hayden approached the
items carefully. The cement around the saw
was coated in sawdust that had been recently

disturbed. But there were no footprints. The person who'd left the items clearly knew what they were doing.

"So the person who took the trophies was wearing a disguise," Carlos said.

"And they ditched it here in the wood shop," Hayden said. "But where did they take the trophies?"

Keisha snapped photos of the items on the table saw. Something must have caught her eye because she leaned forward, peering closely at the mask. "This thing is high quality," she said, poking at it with one finger. "It's not your average Halloween mask."

"It's probably made out of silicone," Jaden explained.

"There's a tag on it." Keisha delicately turned the mask a bit. Hayden thought about stopping her, but she assumed the culprit wouldn't be foolish enough to leave fingerprints all over the mask.

The tag was bright red, with the name of a store written in looping letters on it.

"Hey!" Jaden blurted out. "I recognize that!"

He dug in his pocket and pulled out his deck of cards. On the package was an identical red sticker. "It's from Carter's Magic Emporium," he said.

Keisha placed the mask in another plastic bag from her backpack. "Looks like we're going shopping," she said, heading toward the door.

"Wait!" Hayden stopped her. She checked her watch. "How far away is this place?"

"It's close," Jaden said. "Three blocks, maybe four at the most."

Hayden chewed on her bottom lip and thought it over. Normally, she would never consider leaving the a Math-Tastic competition. However, the deeper the Snoops dug, the more interesting the case became. The trophies had been stolen — and the person who stole them shopped at Carter's Magic Emporium.

"My next round is in forty-five minutes," she said. "So let's hurry."

* * *

The first thing Hayden saw when she walked into Carter's Magic Emporium was the dummy dangling upside-down from the ceiling. It was wrapped in chains, like a magician frozen in mid-escape. The store was decorated with bright red curtains and walls. Rows of long shelves held various masks featuring celebrities, politicians, and cartoon characters. A glass display case housed various small magic tricks.

A lanky man in a black tux waved grandly as the Snoops entered. He wore a tall hat, a pair of black-rimmed glasses, and had a thick mustache that curled at the ends. "Greetings and salutations!" he said. "Welcome to Carter's Magic Emporium! I am Mr. Carter, magician supreme, here to answer your every question about the mystical arts of magic!" He paused. "Well, except how the tricks are done. I can't tell you that."

Jaden immediately rushed over to a giant cabinet stabbed through with several large, dramatic-looking swords. "Whoa," he marveled, trying to pull one of the swords out like King Arthur drawing Excalibur from the stone.

"Better start saving your allowance now, if you want to buy that," Carlos said with a smile.

Hayden approached Mr. Carter. "We're looking for someone who may have shopped here," she said, taking out the plastic bag with the mask in it. "This was purchased at your store."

"Ooooh," Mr. Carter said. "Magic enthusiasts *and* pint-sized detectives. Wonderful!" He took the bag from Hayden and examined the mask. At the sight of it, he fidgeted, turning it over in his hands. "Oh, y-yes," he stammered, "I know this well. It's a —"

A loud crash interrupted him. Hayden spun to see her brother laying on the floor. Jaden was somehow wearing a straitjacket and wrapped in chains, his arms tied behind his back. "Sorry," he said, wiggling around and trying to free himself. "This escape trick is harder than I thought."

"Oh my," Mr. Carter said.

"Lil' help . . . " Jaden groaned, looking like a turtle lying on its back. He squirmed on the floor, unable to stand because of his pinned arms.

Mr. Carter went over and helped him to his feet. "The straitjacket escape is meant for more . . . advanced magicians." With a sweep of his hand, the magician unlocked the jacket and Jaden's arms fell loose. Then with a flourish, he produced from thin air a small kit of keys and handcuffs. "Even Harry Houdini began with the basics," Mr. Carter explained. "You should learn to escape from these

first before moving on to straitjackets and . . . "
He pointed up at the dummy dangling above them.

"Uh, thanks," Jaden said, stripping off the straightjacket.

Mr. Carter returned to Hayden. "As I was saying," he said, becoming frazzled again, "the mask is, well . . . it's fairly common. We sell them year-round, not just at Halloween."

Hayden felt her hopes deflate. "Oh," she said. "So you don't remember anyone purchasing this mask recently?"

Mr. Carter paused one long moment. "I'm . . . afraid not."

Keisha brought up an image of Warren Garvey off the school's social media site. It was a gleaming, smiling photo of him after he won last year's Math-Tastic competition. In his hand was one of the missing trophies. Beside him stood a glum Newt Loggins.

"Have you seen this boy shopping at the store recently?" she asked.

Mr. Carter studied the photo. "Uh, which one?"

"The one holding the trophy," Keisha said.

"No," he said, shaking his head. "I'm sorry."

"No problem," Carlos said. "Thanks anyway."

The Snoops waited while Jaden paid for his
new handcuff set. A dejected Keisha said, "Ugh.
A dead-end. So frustrating. Makes me feel like that
dummy up there, swinging in the wind."

"No worries, Keisha," Carlos said. "Those
trophies couldn't have vanished into thin air. I'm
sure we'll find them."

As they spoke, Hayden watched Mr. Carter
carefully. Something about the way he acted
around the mask wasn't sitting right with her.
She couldn't quite put her finger on it, though.

Suddenly, Hayden's phone chirped. She
gasped. *My meeting with Marple Fan!*

Sure enough, the message was from her
YFC friend.

MARPLE_FAN: *Missed u in the cafeteria.
Find a lead?*

68

Hayden smacked herself upside the head. How could she have been so forgetful?

"Come on," she said, annoyed with herself. "This lead has been anything but magical." Then she shoved open the door to Carter's Magic Emporium and walked out.

CHAPTER 7

THE DISGRACED SUSPECT

SUPERSNOOPER: *A lead, yeah. But it fizzled. Used the Sketch & Arrest app, but the thief was wearing a mask.*

MARPLE_FAN: *No way! The Sketch & Arrest app?! Cooooooooool.*

The Snoops buzzed back to the college. Hayden stood on the pegs of Carlos' dirt bike as he raced down the sidewalk. Jaden, usually a daredevil, pedaled his new bike at a safe speed to avoid falling and scratching the frame or bending the rims. The plastic bag from Carter's Magic Emporium hung from the handlebars. It twisted and turned in the breeze.

They made it back just as several students exited the ballroom and the next group prepared to compete. Hayden entered the ballroom sweaty and disheveled. Miss Kahin saw her and must have noticed her lack of composure.

"Hayden," she said quietly. "Is everything all right?"

"Peachy keen," Hayden said, smoothing her hair. "I'm ready to go."

"Good, because we need you. Do well in this round, and you're a lock for the Countdown Competition final."

"Roger that!" Hayden replied. As she took her seat at one of the desks, she closed her eyes and tried to regain control. This match was important to her. It meant a lot to her team, and to her school. She'd gotten so wrapped up in her Snoops role that she'd lost sight of that.

For this round of the competition, there were twice as many questions and twice as much time to solve them. It was grueling, and Hayden soon found the words and problems getting jumbled in her head. She closed her eyes and focused.

"One problem at a time." Miss Kahin said it all the time. It was the best way to face a test, and the best way to get her mind off the missing trophies.

One problem at a time.

Hayden closed her packet and turned it in with five minutes to go on the clock. She thought she'd done pretty good and had a solid shot at making the Countdown Competition.

Hayden found the other Snoops sitting outside in the grass by the statue. Carlos and Keisha were studying the photos on Keisha's phone of the sawdust trail and the empty trophy case. Jaden was handcuffed and was trying mightily to wriggle his hands to pop the lock on them.

"You know," Carlos said as Hayden shook her head at her brother, "at first I was annoyed by this whole magic thing. But he's been working on freeing himself from those for, like, twenty minutes solid. It's been nice and quiet."

"You know I can hear you, right?" Jaden said, not looking at them. His tongue hung out of his mouth in concentration.

A number of students filled the grassy lawn. It was a perfectly lovely day outside, and many wanted to recharge in the sun, away from the stuffy ballroom. Martin Reynolds had his nose buried in a book titled *The Body in the Library*. Newt Loggins was seated on a bench enjoying a snack.

Frankie Dixon breezed past the Snoops, surrounded by a group of girls. Even without her usual spirit squad friends around her, she'd found followers who wanted to be like her.

"Who arrested *you*?" Frankie Dixon asked Jaden. The girls with her giggled at the joke.

Jaden tried to hide his cuffed hands, but they were bound in front of him. So he turned around, facing away from Frankie. "Just . . . working on my newest magic trick," he said, his voice squeaking. "You'll have to check it out."

"I'm on the edge of my seat," Frankie said sarcastically before disappearing.

Anya Stavos sat in the shade of a tree, texting on her phone. Seeing her made Hayden think about Marple Fan. She wanted to go up to Anya and ask her right there if she was Hayden's online pal. As she watched, Anya set her phone down and began to rummage through her backpack. A look of bewilderment crossed her face. "Where's my practice test?" she asked aloud. "I can't find it anywhere." Martin Reynolds shrugged at her and returned to his reading.

Practice test? Hayden thought of the crumpled-up test the Snoops had found earlier at the scene of the crime. Could it be the same one?

Hayden took a step toward Anya. She was set to ask about the test and if she was also Marple Fan. But then she heard her name being called out behind her.

"Hayden!"

Miss Kahin and several other coaches were exiting the math building. She walked briskly toward the Snoops.

"What's going on?" Keisha asked, but Hayden already knew.

"I made it, didn't I?" she asked.

Miss Kahin nodded eagerly. "You did. You're in the Countdown Competition!"

The other Snoops offered Hayden fist-bumps and high-fives. Jaden tried to hug her, but forgot his hands were still cuffed together. Hayden felt a swell of pride. Despite the craziness of the day, she was still making her team and her teacher proud.

She looked around to see if other students were receiving the same bit of good news. Newt Loggins had a smile plastered on his face. Martin Reynolds was shaking his coach's hand, and Anya Stavos stood with them, jumping for joy. Warren Garvey stood by himself, looking over at —

Warren Garvey?!

She tried to act cool, but he'd startled her. She locked eyes with the former Fleischman mathlete. Warren spun and dashed away, slipping through the nearest door.

"Guys!" Hayden grabbed her brother and swiveled him around. "I just saw Warren Garvey."

"I'm sorry . . . what?" Miss Kahin was baffled.

"No time to explain." Hayden began to run across the lawn. "Come on!"

The four Snoops, including a still-handcuffed Jaden, raced off. Hayden led the way, heading for the door Warren had taken. She swung it open, hurrying inside.

There was no sign of Warren. A few students mingled about. In front of her, the hall split in two. One way led back toward the ballroom, the other led to . . .

"The rec center." She ran off to the left, her sneakers squeaking along the tiled floor. Soon, Keisha was side-by-side with her, making the burst of speed look easy.

The rec center was busier than it had been earlier, with many college students enjoying a bit of lunch. Hayden scanned the crowd, searching for Warren.

"There!" she yelled.

Warren was weaving between students playing pool. He twisted his head back at the sound of Hayden's voice, which was a mistake. One of the pool players drew back her cue and struck Warren right in the stomach.

"Oof!" Warren fell back, hitting another table and scattering the clacking billiard balls.

"Hey!" one of the players on that table shouted. "What's the big idea?"

"Sorry," Warren wheezed.

Hayden and the Snoops reached Warren before he could gather himself and rush off again.

"Warren," Hayden said, facing him head on. "What are you doing here?"

"Yeah," Jaden added, pointing with his cuffed hands. "And where are the trophies? You hid them after you ditched the disguise, didn't you?"

"Jaden, chill." Carlos pressed a hand on Jaden's chest. He redirected his attention to their suspect. "Warren, what are you doing here?"

"I was the star of the team. That trophy was mine. I just wanted another shot at it. And when I was kicked off the team . . . " He trailed off, and it took him a moment to regain his composure.

"Yeah, we get it. You wanted the trophies for yourself. You must have stashed them nearby. So where did you take them?," Jaden asked.

At this, Warren seemed baffled. "Take them?" he asked. "I didn't take them anywhere."

"Come again?" Now it was Jaden's turn to look confused.

"I didn't take the trophies," Warren said. "I would never do that. I respect Math-Tastic too much. I came today because I wanted to know how the team was doing."

"Then why did you run away?" Keisha asked.

"Why wouldn't I?" He toed the carpet with one foot. "I was embarrassed."

"Then if you didn't take the trophies —"
Hayden began. But she didn't get a chance to
finish her thought. Her phone suddenly chirped
in her pocket. She took it out to check, and wasn't
surprised to see a message from Marple Fan.

She was however, surprised to see what the
message was — a photo of the missing trophies!

CHAPTER 8

ANSWER #42

MARPLE_FAN: Haven't you figured it out
yet, Hayden? The answer is #42!

"What does that even mean?" Jaden asked as
he rubbed one of his sore wrists. The handcuffs
he'd been wearing were now back in their small
plastic case and shoved into his hoodie pocket.
"The answer is number forty-two?"

The Snoops were huddled together around Hayden. They stared down in disbelief at the photo and message on her screen. The two trophies sat side by side, resting in a pool of light in an otherwise dark room.

"So this Marple Fan, whoever they are, has been the thief the whole time?" Keisha asked.

Hayden shook her head in disbelief. "It couldn't be her," she said. "Not Marple Fan."

"Why not?" Carlos asked. "What do you really know about this online friend of yours?"

Hayden opened her mouth to answer, but couldn't. What did she know about Marple Fan, anyway? Nothing. Sure, they chatted online, but it was mostly about cases Snoops, Inc. solved, various detection methods, or whatever mystery novels they were reading.

"So you have no idea who this person could be?" Carlos asked her.

"Maybe." Hayden told them about her suspicion that Anya Stavos was actually Marple Fan. "I just never got around to asking her."

"Well, I think we need to go find Anya," Carlos said. "She's our only lead."

"The last place I saw her was in the courtyard," Hayden said, "When she was searching for her practice test."

"Her what?" Keisha had caught the clue the second it slipped from Hayden's lips. She dug the plastic bag from her backpack.

"Her practice test." Hayden took the bag containing the crumpled test and looked it over. "Anya must be Marple Fan."

"So she dropped her test when she stole the trophies," Carlos deduced.

"And left a trail of sawdust in the lobby," Hayden said. "Remember, she walked past us right before we discovered the messy carpet."

It all made sense, except for how Anya seemed like such a nice girl. They had so much in common and had hit it off right away. Why would Anya snatch the trophies? What was her motive?

"I say we find this Anya girl and get some answers once and for all," Jaden said.

"Hmmm, answers . . . " Hayden sat at the nearest table. She dug a sucker from her backpack. Strawberry this time. She'd already eaten all her favorite grape suckers. She repeated the word, over and over. "Answer . . . answer . . . the answer is number forty-two."

Hayden unzipped the plastic bag with the practice test and reached inside for it. "Hey!" Jaden said. "I thought that was evidence."

"We were supposed to find it," Hayden said, smoothing the test flat on the table. No name was written on it. But the looping letters and numbers in the margins looked like a girl's writing. It was Anya's practice test, for sure. She'd only started it, too. Only the first page was finished.

Hayden found question number forty-two on the third page.

Scribbled next to it was a smiley face with the words, *Hi Snoops, Incorporated!*

"Bingo," Hayden said.

"Whoa," Jaden whispered over her shoulder.

Question forty-two was a word problem. It read:

42. Mikey the Squirrel is gathering acorns for winter. If he gathers an average of 31 acorns in four hours, and an average of 30 acorns in five hours, how many acorns did Mikey collect in the fifth hour?

She grabbed a pen out of her backpack and went to work.

Jaden, who also read the problem, muttered, "Ouch. My brain hurts."

"Well, nothing out of the ordinary there," Carlos said with a smile.

Hayden scratched numbers on the test paper. She first figured out the number of acorns in the first four hours by multiplying. "31 times 4 equals 124," she said, her sucker dancing in her mouth as she spoke. She then determined how many acorns were gathered in hour five, and subtracted the two totals. "30 times 5 equals 150. Take the difference of 150 minus 124, and you get . . . "

She wrote the answer in the blank and circled it. "26!" she cried.

Hayden looked up at the other Snoops. Their expressions hadn't changed.

"Okay," Jaden said. "You're smart. Good job. But what does twenty-six mean? Why is it a clue?"

Keisha looked toward the far wall of the rec center. Next to the large bulletin board was a map of the school. "What if number twenty-six isn't a what?" she puzzled out. "What if it's a where?"

Hayden wasn't sure what she was talking about. How could a number be a place? But when she followed Keisha to the map, it made sense.

The overhead map of the school showed every building, every level, every hall. There was even a cute little waving figure standing in the map's rec center, with a word balloon that said, "Hey! I'm right here!" To the left of the map was a list of every classroom in the school. Each was coded with a number.

Keisha scanned for room 26. As she did, something on the bulletin board caught Jaden's attention. He pulled a flyer down off the wall. "Cool," he said. "A kid magician. Maybe he can teach me a few things." He held the flyer out for Hayden to see.

Hayden started to swat it away but stopped. "Wait a second," she said. "Is that . . .?"

"Got it!" Keisha pumped a fist in the air and pointed to the directory. There *was* a room 26. Hayden's eyes went from the flyer to the map and back again.

And just like that — *Abracadabra!* — the solution to the whole mystery appeared.

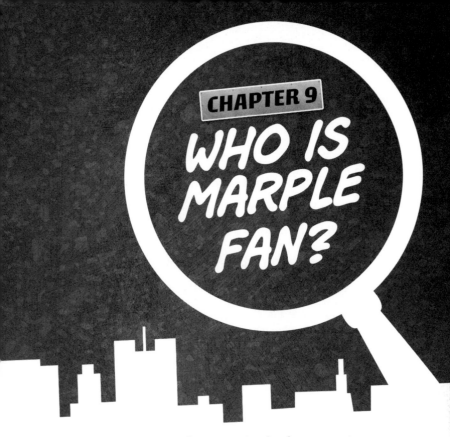

CHAPTER 9

WHO IS MARPLE FAN?

Room 26 was, of course, in the basement of the math building. Where there were no windows . . . or sunlight . . . or sound.

So, basically the creepiest part of the college, Hayden thought. *Figures.*

A row of fluorescent bulbs lined the ceiling. They hummed and buzzed as the Snoops made their way down the hall and finally reached the room they were looking for.

"Room 26," Hayden said, pointing to the sign on the door. She read it aloud. "Boiler Room."

"Come on." Keisha shoved past Jaden and Carlos. With one hand, she pushed the heavy metal door wide open. It creaked and groaned, almost like it was warning them of danger.

"Hello?" Hayden called out into the darkness. She could hear the boiler inside grumbling, the air temperature rising and thickening. "Is anybody in here?"

There was no answer.

As she stepped into the boiler room, a glint of glittering gold caught her eye.

"The trophies!"

They sat side by side under the glow of a single light bulb dangling above them. Relief and excitement washed over Hayden. Finally, the trophies could be taken back to the Math-Tastic competition, just in time for the final round.

A sudden burst of clapping erupted from behind them. Hayden's heart leapt into her throat and held fast.

"Congratulations, Snoops, Inc.," a voice said. "You've done it again."

Hayden and the other Snoops turned around to see a silhouette framed in the doorway. The figure stepped forward . . .

"Martin Reynolds?" Jaden exclaimed.

A smile stretched across the quiet Watson student's face.

"Hold up," Keisha said. "You're Marple Fan? But Miss Marple is a woman."

Martin chuckled. "Nope . . . it's all misdirection."

"He's not only Marple Fan," Hayden said, holding up the flyer. "He's also The Magnificent Martinelli!"

The flyer Jaden had found on the bulletin board showed a young magician in a full tuxedo. His arms were raised, a top hat held in one hand. Wisps of smoke wrapped around him. The young magician was unmistakably Martin.

"Bravo," Martin said. "You caught me!" He waved his hands in one fluid movement, and a pair of handcuffs appeared around his wrists.

"Whoa!" Jaden looked impressed. "Coooool."

"You know," Martin said. "It's been fun to watch you all day . . . while hiding in plain sight. But the best part had to be describing the so-called 'trophy thief' for you. You guys bought into that way too easily." He laughed. "See, Hayden has always told me how good the Snoops crew is. I just had to see for myself."

"So wait," Carlos said. "This has all been . . .?"

"One big game?" Martin's smile grew wider, if possible. "Yep."

"And we followed your clues perfectly," Hayden said. "You stole the trophies and snuck off to the wood shop, making sure you were seen."

Carlos took over. "You hid them here, then put Anya's practice test where we would find it."

"Then you through the lobby," Hayden said. "Making sure to wipe your dirty sneakers on the carpet and leave a trail of sawdust."

Keisha took over. "You pretended you saw the thief and described him for us because you knew we'd find your disguise."

"Which led us to Carter's Magic Emporium," Jaden concluded, adding, "Super awesome store, by the way."

"You nailed it," Martin said. "Yeah. I told Mr. Carter to act cool if someone came asking about me."

"So that's why he was acting so funny," Hayden said.

"But wait," Jaden said. "The glass case was locked. How did you even snatch the trophies?"

"My trusty trick handcuff kit," Martin said. "Mr. Carter sold it to me the first time I shopped at the store. Picks any lock."

"Hey!" Jaden smiled proudly. "I just bought one of those!"

"Pretty elaborate chase you had us on today," Carlos said.

"And here you are." Martin gestured grandly at the twin trophies bathed in light. As he did, the handcuffs binding his wrists together magically disappeared. "You found the trophies. Nicely done."

Hayden checked her watch. "Yeah, and not a moment too soon," she said. "The Countdown Competition is going to start in fifteen minutes. We both better get moving, Martin."

"Good call," Martin said, picking up the trophies. "I'll just take these back to where they belong."

The Watson student was the first to reach the door. But as he walked by, he kicked out the small piece of wood under the door that was propping it open. "Oops, clumsy me!" he said as the door began to creak closed.

"Stop the door!" Hayden shouted.

"Can't," Martin said slyly. "Kind of got my hands full."

The last thing the Snoops saw before the boiler room door slammed closed and locked was Martin smiling at them.

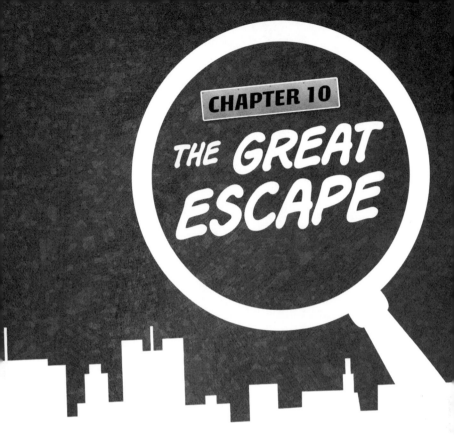

CHAPTER 10

THE *GREAT* ESCAPE

Boom!

The boiler room was thrown into darkness. The only light left came from the bulb hanging above where the trophies had just been sitting.

"He . . . he just . . . " Jaden couldn't form words. He stared at the closed door.

Keisha tried the door handle. "Locked," she said, twisting it more vigorously. Then she slammed her shoulder into the door and yelled, "Hey! Open up!"

There was no response. Keisha continued to pound her fists on the door. The sound rippled like thunder in the enclosed space.

Jaden looked at the flyer in his hand. "Magnificent Martinelli? Pfft! Hardly!" He crumpled up the paper and tossed it to the dirty floor.

The image of the Magnificent Martinelli gave Hayden an idea. "Jaden," she said, "Where's that handcuff kit of yours?"

"Now's not the time for me to practice," Jaden said. "We have to get you out of here."

Hayden rolled her eyes. "Just give it to me."

Jaden plopped the small kit into his sister's hand. Hayden knelt in front of the locked door.

"Houdini's not the only one with mad escape skills," Hayden said as she plucked two items out of the case. One was a long, slender pick; the other was an L-shaped tension wrench. They were similar to the ones she had in her lock-pick kit at home. Using the wrench, Hayden pressed down on the keyhole. Then she inserted the pick and felt her way through the tumblers.

Two minutes later, and . . . *Click!*

The boiler room door swung open.

"Nice work!" Carlos said. He gave her a high-five as the team took off down the creepy basement hallway.

When they reached the main hall again, Hayden checked her watch. "Two minutes!" she shouted. The Countdown Competition was about to start!

Bursting into the lobby, Hayden saw several of the competition officials standing by the trophy case. They held the newly-found trophies and spoke happily with one another.

Hayden threw open the closed door of the ballroom. The crowd inside turned to see who had made the dramatic entrance. Tuam and Miss Kahin's eyes went wide.

"Hurry!" Miss Kahin said, waving her in. "You need to be seated before the test begins."

Hayden dashed for the stage and slid into an open desk just as the official announced, "Let the Countdown Competition begin!"

Hayden looked over and saw Martin seated nearby. He was scowling at her. She simply waved and smiled at the jerk.

While Hayden concentrated on the final round of questions, the other Snoops approached Miss Kahin. Hayden tried not to focus on them, but at one point, she heard her coach audibly gasp.

There's no way the Magnificent Martinelli will escape from this, Hayden thought with a chuckle.

* * *

"Don't worry, you got this." Jaden whispered words of encouragement in his sister's ear as he shuffled his deck of playing cards.

The Fleischman Math-Tastic team was seated in the ballroom, waiting for the awards to be handed out. Miss Kahin had allowed Jaden, Carlos, and Keisha to join them. Back in the crowd, Hayden could see her mom seated with the rest of the parents.

After the Countdown Competition, the Snoops team told the officials all they knew about the missing trophies. Hayden spared no detail, even showing them the photo of the trophies that Martin Reynolds had sent her. When she was done, Martin was disqualified and led away by the officials.

"If I may have your attention," a woman on stage said into a microphone. "We have the results. First, I'd like to thank the bold group of kids who helped find our misplaced trophies. Thank you all."

The crowd politely applauded.

"Now, the exciting part. Taking first place in the individual competition is . . . "

Hayden held her breath.

"Hayden Williams, Fleischman Middle School!"

Hayden leaped from her chair as the crowd burst into applause. Tuam gave her a giant bear hug, lifting her off the ground. Miss Kahin was beaming with pride.

"I knew you could do it," Jaden said. "Good work, sis."

"Way to go," Keisha said.

"Smartest Snoop I know," Carlos said.

From her spot with the Watson team, Anya Stavos gave Hayden a smile and a thumbs-up.

The official continued. "And the team award for this year's Math-Tastic regional competition is — Fleischman Middle School!"

Another huge round of applause filled the ballroom. Miss Kahin led the team onto the stage, where they accepted their trophies. Hayden hefted her individual trophy into the air. Soon, her name would join the list of winners on the trophy, forever holding a spot in Math-Tastic history.

"Woo-hoo!" The other Snoops joined the team on stage. As they did, Jaden excitedly flung his deck of playing cards up into the sky. They drifted down like confetti, making the kids and everyone in the audience laugh.

Jaden looked down at the scattered cards. "Uh . . . anybody wanna play Fifty-Two Card Pick-Up?"

THE END

■ Snoops, Inc. Case Report #004

Prepared by Hayden Williams

THE CASE:

Find the pair of Math-Tastic trophies someone snatched right before the competition began.

CRACKING THE CASE:

Little did I know that the regional Math-Tastic competition would turn into a huge mystery to find a pair of missing trophies. When it came to finding a suspect, I used the new Sketch & Arrest app to make a composite sketch.

Police often bring along forensic sketch artists when they interview witnesses or victims of crimes. They first ask people to choose from a range of sample eyes, noses, mouths, and other features. The artist then draws an image of a suspect or missing person based on the witness's description.

Facial composites were used as far back as the 1880s. Alphonse Bertillon first developed a system of using facial features taken from photos. Today sketch artists usually use computer software and applications to do the same thing.

I *love* this stuff. I could talk about it all day. Anyway, Sketch & Arrest was only one key piece of the mystery, but it definitely helped us to . . .

CRACK THE CASE!_

WHAT DO YOU THINK?

1. Anya was very friendly toward Hayden right away. Did this make you suspicious of Anya? Or did you believe her friendly behavior was genuine? Discuss why you chose your answer.

2. During her test, Hayden remembers Miss Kahin's motto: "One problem at a time." How does this relate to Hayden's situation? Has there ever been a time in your life when these words would have been helpful?

3. Martin's reason for choosing Marple Fan as his online name was "misdirection." What do you think he means by this?

WRITE YOUR OWN!

1. Close your eyes and imagine one of your close friends or family members. Now try to describe or draw them from memory. How closely does your mental image of this person look like the real person?

2. Hayden is dealing with several events in this story. Write about a time when you had to juggle more than one thing at a time, and how you handled the pressure to succeed.

3. Say you've decided to become a magician. Create a name for your act, and design a trick you would use to dazzle your audience.

GLOSSARY

CONTAMINATED (kuhn-TA-muh-nay-tuhd)—dirty or unfit for use

CULPRIT (KUHL-prit)—someone who is guilty of doing something wrong or of committing a crime

LANYARD (LAN-yurd)—a strap or cord worn around the neck to which an ID badge or other objects can be attached

MOTIVE (MOH-tiv)—a reason for doing something

OBNOXIOUS (uhb-NOK-shuhss)—very unpleasant, annoying, or offensive

SILHOUETTE (sil-oo-ET)—an outline of something that shows its shape

SILICONE (SIL-ih-kohn)—a soft, flexible material often used for making masks and disguises

STAKEOUT (STAKE-out)—a situation in which someone watches a place to look for suspicious activity

SUSPECT (SUHSS-pekt)—someone thought to be responsible for a crime

ABOUT THE AUTHOR

Brandon Terrell has been a lifelong fan of mysteries, shown by his collection of nearly 200 Hardy Boys books. He is the author of numerous children's books, including several titles in series such as Tony Hawk's 900 Revolution, Jake Maddox Graphic Novels, Spine Shivers, and Sports Illustrated Kids: Time Machine Magazine.

When not hunched over his laptop, Brandon enjoys watching movies and television, reading, watching and playing baseball, and spending time at home with his wife and two children in Minnesota.

ABOUT THE ILLUSTRATOR

Mariano Epelbaum is an experienced character designer, illustrator, and traditional 2D animator. He has been working as a professional artist since 1996, and enjoys trying different art styles and techniques.

Throughout his career Mariano has created many expressive characters and designs for a wide range of films, TV series, commercials, and publications in his native country of Argentina. In addition to Snoops, Inc., Mariano has also contributed to the Fairy Tale Mixups and You Choose: Fractured Fairy Tales series for Capstone.

FOLLOW THE **SNOOPS** INC.
TEAM AS THEY FIND THE
CLUES AND CRACK ALL
THEIR CASES!

*BE SURE TO TRACK DOWN AND READ ALL
OF THE SNOOPS, INC. MYSTERIES!*

THE FUN DOESN'T STOP THERE! LEARN MORE ABOUT THE
SNOOPS CREW AT *WWW.CAPSTONEKIDS.COM.*